SOULMATES

A Play about Love and Deceit

By

Philipp J. Caesar

Table of Contents

The Author: About Myself

I'm Phil and I'm a film producer, actor, social media influencer, song writer, musician and trainer.

With education in compassionate acting in Los Angeles, Munich, London and New York with world leading coaches such as Susan Batson (Susan Batson Studio, NY), Lisa Haisha (Soul Blazing, LA) and Bernard Hiller (Acting and Success Studio, LA) and James Kemp (Room one, London) I have authored a number of scripts for theatre and films, composed and published numerous songs for versatile genres.

Having taken many decisive routes as an artist and in successfully battling resistance to create, I have discovered that to empower someone, I as the artist must be empowered myself.

My philosophy is to sincerely inspire and empower my audience to believe in themselves and to make strong choices while staying centered. Being true to oneself and maintaining a level of calm, is the most valuable asset.

I live by : "Meditate, don't hate, visualize, recreate."

SOULMATES

Scenes 1 to 24

IN THREE ACTS

Act I

1.   EXT. OUTSIDE ON A TERASSE OF A BIG MANSION

Arthur and Elizabeth are both guests at a party of a very rich producer. They both don't know each other and are both going outside to take a breath of fresh air. Arthur wants to be a professional Hollywood actor and Elisabeth is attempting a professional career as a dancer. Both are single. Music is playing in the background. There is still a calming silence in the air. There is an amazing freshness in the air. Elisabeth is reaching for a cigarette wanting to light it but her lighter doesn't work. Arthur approaches her with a lighter.

Party music in the distant and nature atmosphere.

> ARTHUR
> Your precious form of golden dust the way
> you move fills me with lust.

He ignites the lighter, holds a minute and then attempts to kiss her but she pushes him away and slaps his cheek.

> ELIZABETH
> How dare you speak these vulgar words you are
> raging like an outlawed turd.

> ARTHUR
> More like an eagle full of strength, endurance
> and enormous length.

> ELIZABETH
> You men are truly all the same
> your sexist talk fills me with shame. Your
> hormones they tear me apart
> will someone ever speak with heart.

> ARTHUR
> Mistaken surely you must be
> the pathway to your destiny
> just opened with intensity.
> I surely am your remedy.

> ELIZABETH
> You touch me it's a felony
> and you will face my weaponry.

> ARTHUR
> What would life be without the touch
> of loving souls to bond and such.

> ELIZABETH

Before I trust you with my breast
you need to pass a loyal test.

ARTHUR
Is love the kind you seek to gain?

ELIZABETH
Oh, love it is a dream in vain, for all it
does Is create pain.

ARTHUR
No, hear it's love that heals the mind,
it nurtures and it makes us shine.
It helps us trust and feel at peace,
through celebrating the release.

ELIZABETH
You go your way and I will see
if you're the man that goes with me.

ARTHUR
I'm here right now so don't you see that you
and me are meant to be?

ELIZABETH
The only thing I need is time,
so wait for me and stand in line.

ARTHUR
The line I'll cross the world is wild,
let's find what I shall win and grind.

Arthur exits

Blackout

2. BAR LATE NIGHT

Arthur is love-struck, motivated and feels very confident that he is going to win Elisabeth's heart. He sits at the table with a clear view on an empty seated piano that is right next to his table. He hums a melody fantasizing being with her. He imagines himself with her holding hands running down the beach. The bar is empty. He takes a last sip of his gin tonic, gets up and sits down at the piano and starts playing. He plays the song Cherie. When he finishes with his song he realizes that the bar has filled and people start applauding.

                    ARTHUR

        Thank you, thank you. Thanks.

He gets up from the piano and approaches the bar and suddenly Elisabeth is standing right next to him.

                    ELIZABETH
        Suspiciously you have that smile
        now did you find something to
        grind?

                    ARTHUR
        A lot of women came to me
        and asked me for a symphony
        but I refused...
        cause in my mind
        you are the very one to grind.

                    ELIZABETH
        Your charming talk it makes me feel
        a hurricane it feels surreal

                    ARTHUR
        It is the realest of all real,
        now can't you feel I'm the real deal.

                    ELIZABETH
        I need more proof not only dust,
        the only thing I see is lust.
        How could I ever give you trust
        for love you're failing to adjust?

    Arthur is getting frustrated.

                    ARTHUR
        What is there to adjust, let´s go,

stop acting like a little hoe.

ELIZABETH
What did you say?!!!!!
I'll burst your brain and smash your lung
that you´ll think twice to use your tongue.

ARTHUR
Oh, Jesus...
all I meant to say...
you have a very special way
and sure the least of things you play
is stubbornly obey.

ELIZABETH
You're saying I'm a stubborn prude
I'll call the guards that you intrude.

ARTHUR
Now wait a moment and relax
the opposite I'm telling you.
So many magic things to do.
I see you are a wife of class
and to your ass, I lift my glass.

ELIZABETH
Enough I'm going to call the guards
and you'll be banned a thousand yards.

ARTHUR
Please listen you misunderstand,
I'm here because I am your fan.

ELIZABETH
Help!!!!

ARTHUR
Relax!!!!

ELIZABETH
Help me !!!!

Arthur backs off and drops his last line

ARTHUR
You and me could really be
and I will call YOU my Cherie.

Arthur rushes away

3. INT. HER CHAMBER STAGE RIGHT

Elisabeth is sitting in the bathtub. She is seemingly longing to be with someone. She is longing for the love she so deeply craves inside of her heart. There is a numbing silence in the air. Her children are at their fathers. She reaches for the red wine glass that is standing next to the bathtub tab. She takes a huge sip to wash down her pain. She makes a big sigh.

> ELIZABETH
> What have I done, I like this man,
> I feel I'm strong, I know I can.
> Now please, dear God, give me a sign
> so I can have him just as mine.
> I can't be living in the past.
> The present I want, I want life,
> a joyful world full of surprise.
> I hope that he will find the card
> and he will call and we can start.

4. INSIDE HIS CHAMBER

Arthur devastated by the rejection decided to get drunk. He sits down on a chair. All over his apartment he has Buddha statues. Everywhere are empty incense packages and Lotus flowers. We get the impression that he is deeply spiritual. He actively is seeking redemption in calming down and being in the moment to visualize being with her despite her previous rejection towards him.

> ARTHUR
> How else do I now make her see,
> to get her sleep and be with me?
> Why is it always so obscene
> the slightest touch to cause a scene.
> ...The liquor yeah, it numbs the pain,
> new strength my heart is meant to gain.

Grabs a cigarette. Finds a business card in his cigarette pack and realizes it's her contacts. He drops down to his knees praising God.

> ARTHUR
> Thank you dear mighty force
> of the universe...!!!
> No way. Dear awesome life of sin,
> I love it, let the show begin.

5. CONVERSATION OVER PHONE STAGE LEFT STAGE RIGHT

He is sitting in front of his Buddha statue with a burning incense and she is still in her bathtub.

                    ELIZABETH
Hello?

            ARTHUR
I want to make it up to you,
a dance in red and I'm in blue.

                    ELIZABETH
A dance?

            ARTHUR
Yes, a dance to prove my loyalty with
manner and with extasy.

                ELIZABETH
This one last chance I give to you,
now   choose the place to meet, us two.

            ARTHUR
Let's meet us at the riverbank
at 9 pm to make me thank.

                ELIZABETH
Your luck   is that you made that choice
my favorite is the river´s voice..

                ARTHUR
That's why I chose this awesome place
so we can play like sharks and rays.

                ELIZABETH
You truly are a charming man,
and you said that you are my fan?

                ARTHUR
Much more I am than just your fan And, full
of manners yes...I can.

                ELIZABETH
Your manners they're one of a kind

                ARTHUR
You are the girl I seek to find

11

                    ELIZABETH
        Oh, charming, charming wizardtalk.
        I'll see you there, it's a long walk.

They hang up the phone. Arthur jumps around

                    ARTHUR
        yeas, yeah, yeah, yeah, I'm the
        maaaaaannnnnn

        Blackout

6. EXT. AT THE RIVERBANK

Elisabeth is already at the Riverbank. It seems like she is casting a voodoo spell. She takes a Fruit and throws it into the river. The river is like a mirror. There is an amazing Zenlike calmness in the air. The splash of the fruit is breaking the mirror. Right at that moment Arthur approaches with a rose in his hand. She turns around.

                    ELIZABETH
        Now show me that you speak the truth or is
        it naive speaking youth?

He grabs her and they start dancing tango.

                    ARTHUR
        Direct an honest I speak truth,
        my heart wants you, my eyes are proof.
        I tell you all it is a mess
        that hasn't started with the flesh.

                    ELIZABETH
        What is it always 'bout the flesh, cannot
        believe it is the best.

                    ARTHUR
        Now once our spirits fly and play
        we'll reach the height in night and day and
        everything will fall in place
        in healing and devine new ways.

                    ELIZABETH
        Now all these shining things you say,
        how do you know so well to play?

ARTHUR
For lawful carnal practice chess,
I studied with the very best.

ELIZABETH
Oh, chess I know but what you say
speaks pleasure and aroused cliché

ARTHUR
It might sound as if it's passé
the finest technique oui...olé

ELIZABETH
Oh yes, I want to give my flesh
to someone with such manly chest,
but hold a moment and sign here,
whenever I'm in fear you're near.

ARTHUR
With ease, with ease, now patience please,
let's slowly start with tease and squeeze.

ELIZABETH
You sign right here and all you get
is finest scent and my pure flesh.

ARTHUR
Another way to find the key to limitless infinity...
Must be in sight now let it be.
I got to go and you will see
my proof way more than loyalty.

He rushes out and runs away.

Blackout

7. IN THE STREET

Arthur is walking down an ally. Everywhere graffiti is sprayed all over the walls. Light is shining from the top. It seems like he is in a tunnel of gold. It has an atmosphere of the final walk to light. Towards redemption.

> ARTHUR
> A contract oh dear lord tell me
> why can´t you let me living free. Insane
> she wants to make me sign
> a bond to be, where is the wine!?

Beat

> Now tell me why you run away that
> woman wants to give her flesh to you
> and you resign?
> Forget about the fear and sign!

Act II

8. INT. AT THE BAR

Elisabeth is sitting alone on the couch at the bar where Arthur played the song on the piano. She has the same facial impression she had when she was in the bathtub. Clearly longing for love. She is fighting the defeat. Jazz music is playing in the background. Suddenly Arthur approaches her.

> ARTHUR
> Your face it feels like roses
> welcomed by the sun.
> The everlasting force that
> glorifies existence.

> ELIZABETH
> Who speaks that sound of healing wind?

> ARTHUR
> Forgive woman for I have sinned.

> ELIZABETH
> What have you done oh, mystic child!

> ARTHUR
> I got so drunk and acted wild

He throws his jacket next to her.

> ELIZABETH
> Don't tell me you have touched some flesh.

> ARTHUR
> For I don't grasp the thought in mind it has
> been poison of some kind.

> ELIZABETH
> Your lies they cannot stand for good. You're
> driven by the devil´s hood
> that voice you darely temper.

> ARTHUR
> The oath I swear. My words are pure. A lot
> of liquor I endure.
> And this time I would think of you at
> everything I went to do.

She throws the jacket at him.

ELIZABETH
You pack your fur and out with you, for
granted you take what I do
so I don't have no use for you
the truth I want now tell me who?

She seemingly demands an answer. Instantly he drops to his knees.
She is truly shocked because she didn't expect his sudden change.

ARTHUR
My words are pure so hear
the truth I swear I'm clear
and not confused.
My wife I want you, you and me
united for eternity.

Reaches a ring out of a vending machine.

ELIZABETH
Is that the truth you speak to me.
You really want the sacred we?
Is it the liquor speaking shame
the words you charmingly use to claim.

ARTHUR
My heart I reach towards your heart, my soul
and from my closest parts with loyalty of
righteous kind, devine creation you shall find

ELIZABETH
Oh, dearest handsome wonder male, I
knew our love it will prevail.
Let's make a baby here and now, I'm
fertile let's begin the vow.

ARTHUR
Oh, woman so the truth to speak, were
rising to the highest peak, for you and me a
bond indeed together our minds are freed.

He kisses her, she backs off, gets up and runs off

ARTHUR
Jesus. What is it now again .....
I need to show my heart to her a song to rise and
shine and she would dance around me like a
panther. Telling her how much I care, how much I
love her sweetest scent that I want her to keep an
everlasting smile to always reach the highest
heights. That when it's dark she'll see the light

and we would never have to fight.
I know that she'll be back at the bar,
so I shall bring the sky and stars.

Blackout

9. INT. IN THE BAR LATE AT NIGHT

Arthur is sitting at the piano again. He is seemingly love drunk and is playing the song "Rise and Shine". Once he played the last note he sees her and approaches her.

ELIZABETH
Oh, such a lovely song and rhyme now
simply come with me and sign

ARTHUR
I swear we should unite and lime
and we don't have to sign this time.

ELIZABETH
I thought you are a special kind
with doubt you start to fill my mind.

ARTHUR
I need to live I can't be bound
I want to dance and feel the sound.

ELIZABETH
If you want me I need to see
that you're sincere so sign the plea!

ARTHUR
Can't have these shackles that suppress
I need your scent and love not less.

ELIZABETH
You'll get much more I'll love you blind, my scent,
my heart and mind combined.

ARTHUR
Extortion that's just what this is,
this will not stand I am a wiz

ELIZABETH
If you don't go with what I claim
for someone else I need to aim.
I don't have time for childlike games
that temper's doomed to burn in flames.

ARTHUR
I can't believe you speak such hate.
I know my love is strong and great.

ELIZABETH
A wizard you are that's what's up, I think
you better leave and stop.

ARTHUR
Now wait a second and hear me,
what happened, you and me Cherie?

ELIZABETH
Don't ever say that I'm your cherry
just lay down on the cemetery
so I can find someone to marry.
Your stupid song
it just feels wrong.

Arthur's heart is literally breaking as if he had just gotten stabbed.

ARTHUR
I see, you send away a love
that channels light right from above.
Can't hold that longing for your love
I'll nevcr comc back I am off.

Arthur devastated runs off

ELIZABETH
Wait!!!!!!!

Blackout

10. ARTHUR GETTING DRUNK ON A CLIFF

Arthur is standing on a thirty meter tall cliff. The ocean is wild and there is a cold piercing wind blowing. In his left hand he holds a cigarette and in the other one he is holding a bottle of vodka. One can really feel the unpredictable force of nature. If he were to fall, he would lose his life.

Totally wasted

>   ARTHUR
> I can play these games as well.
> Nothing but a little hoe
> I give my heart to her
> and show my passion all along
> and I get as if I did wrong.
> It's cause she simply hates us
> men. Don´t want to live if I can´t
> have what she does not want me
> to have.
> I make it quick and I get drunk
> and find the courage now to
> jump.

Elizabeth stands behind him.

>   ELIZABETH
> Don't jump!

Arthur seemingly shocked

>   ARTHUR
> What do you want?
> You want to push me like a thief
> and make me bleed out on the reef?

>   ELIZABETH
> No listen you are drunk and wild
> Now come with me, relax my
> child.

>   ARTHUR
> Now watch your mouth, I am not a child!!!!
> I might be powerful and wild
> but you don't want my life of art
> so I'd be doomed shall life restart.

Steps forward closes his eyes and gets ready to jump.

>   ELIZABETH

20

Don't jump, oh please, don't jump away, I loved
that you have crossed my way.

ARTHUR
Lies and lies just games and games
Now praise the liquor and the way that I
will fly and fade away.

Holds up the bottle but she grabs it.

ARTHUR
What are you doing, give it back!

ELIZABETH
I want you to come back to life
I need to see your sober eyes.

ARTHUR
You'll never see my eyes again
give me my liquor back and then
I'll jump to death and I would be
away from pain and blasphemy.

He grabs the bottle but she pulls it away. He is so drunk that he falls to the
ground.

ELIZABETH
Oh, please come back oh mystic child
I need your bliss the way you smiled.

ARTHUR
The way I smiled, now anytime I smile at you
you say I'm vulgar and confused.

ELIZABETH
I said that cause you've touched my butt.

ARTHUR
When did I ever touch your butt
manipulation, scam and lord knows what.

ELIZABETH
Don't want to argue what you did
just come with me, let's talk a bit.

ARTHUR
You'll never see my face again....
I love you...no I hate your guts ...
my heart it burst, my veins they pop,

another liquor in my cart
and I shall finish what I start.

He tumbles off. She stays back. She takes a big sip.

> ELIZABETH
> Oh, Jesus that heart is a mess
> he must have cared about me yes.
> Now how do I now make him see
> that I indeed want him with me.
>
> He must be different than all men that
> have abused me way back then. And now
> I've torn his heart apart
> I love his music and his art.
>
> I need to find him in his trance
> to get him back and even dance.

Blackout

11. STREET CORNER ARTHUR IS LYING ON THE STREET

It is early in the morning. The birds and roosters are screaming. Arthur is lying on a bench, sleeping out his high. There is an unbarring heat. Elizabeth is looking everywhere and finally finds him. In one end he has his empty vodka bottle and in the other hand he has his ukulele. She approaches him and wakes him up.

> ELIZABETH
> Hey handsome

Arthur wakes up, is looking around wondering how he got there.

> ARTHUR
> Oh, hey!

> ELIZABETH
> Thank God your eyes are clear again.

> ARTHUR
> Clearer than when?

> ELIZABETH
> Then, last night at the ocean wall?

> ARTHUR
> Give me a hint I don't recall.

22

ELIZABETH
Don't worry and just play your song
to make you see that I was wrong.
The truth is that I love your song.

He smiles and starts playing the song. As the song is finished.

ARTHUR
Amazing...that was more than fine, now tell
me where do I now sign?

Blackout

12. INT. IN THE BEDROOM WAKING UP IN SHOCK

Arthur is waking up in shock full of sweat. One can see in his eyes that he is
deeply longing to be safe. Private moment. He washes his face and Elizabeth is
entering the room coked up. He is simply about to lose it.

ARTHUR
I got to tell you, I love you and I want to
support you wherever I can but I feel
neglected and I don't know whether I can live
with that.

ELIZABETH
I told you that I have to take care of these
things. I can't just leave everything behind.

ARTHUR
Keep everything you enjoy doing. I want you
to make choices.

ELIZABETH
I love you. It's a very difficult time for me and
I have to take care of my children, my taxes.

ARTHUR
I understand that. However, I have needs
and you do not fulfill them.

ELIZABETH
I am sorry. I don't have time for this now.
I need to take care of important things.
You should have gotten it more clear instead
you are getting stoned and are not working.

ARTHUR
Hearing the alcoholic speaking.

ELIZABETH
I don't have time for drama.

ARTHUR
What is it always about the drama? How are
we ever going to get to know each other if we
can't even have a normal conversation
talking about things that are actually going
on in our lives? I want to be happy and I
wanna have a great future.

ELIZABETH
I want to be happy too. I booked a session for
a couple´s meeting. So, we can learn how to
communicate better.

ARTHUR
Tonight? I thought we were gonna go to the
movies tonight. ....
Great. I mean. That's so great.

ELIZABETH
No if you don't want it we won't go.

ARTHUR
No okay we are going. I can't wait to be
inspired by a couple retreat.

ELIZABETH
And then you can start hanging around with
people that are not good for you.

ARTHUR
Inspired, I am getting already darling. Oh
darlingueeee.

ELIZABETH
Are you okay?

ARTHUR
What are we for you? I mean what is this?

We see each other maybe
9   days a month and when we see each
other we are fighting all the time as soon as
we are actually opening up to one another
talking about something real.

ELIZABETH
This is all new for me I'm sorry that I am
such a terrible girlfriend.

ARTHUR
Jesus. Why are you talking like this?
I am simply saying that I feel that my needs
are not met here.
I need stimuli.
I want us to be together.
I want to see you once in a while.
I want to know who you are.
I want you to talk about your feelings.

ELIZABETH
Ha ha... My feelings, I doubt that you are
able to handle that. You are a man.

ARTHUR
What is this supposed to mean?

ELIZABETH
Well it means all you care about is your dick
and as soon as another woman comes around
I am not interesting to you any longer because
you wanna fuck anything that moves.

ARTHUR
How would you know that?
Oh yeah because I treat you like shit, right?
It's because I'm sacrificing my precious time,
that nobody is going to pay me back by the
way, sitting in my car for 12 hours to come to
be with you, playing daddy, driving you
around helping you to take care of your
paperwork, finding solutions to problems
that aren't even mine.

ELIZABETH
Well, I didn't ask you to solve my problems.

ARTHUR
Oh my God, can't you see that I am
helping you because I love you and I

25

don't want you to have any problems.

ELIZABETH
Ha... You are a great manipulator.
I saw the way you looked at Catherine.
I know what you're doing.
It's always the same.

ARTHUR
Who?

ELIZABETH
Don't play dumb here!

ARTHUR
Catherine... Who? You are insane!

ELIZABETH
I can't talk now. I have to work.

ARTHUR
I understand that, take all the space
you need. But this is an important
thing and I want to talk about this.

ELIZABETH
It's difficult to talk about my feelings
and there's so much to do,
I don't even know where to start.
I am a mother and I have to get these
things sorted out.
Please, I can't do all these things at
once. I need to get them done.

ARTHUR
Well, that's just great. I don't
think this is going to work.

He grabs a bottle of whiskey and starts walking away.

ELIZABETH
Where are you going?

ARTHUR
I'm going out, finding a place to think,
getting my head straight, thinking about my
precious future.

ELIZABETH

About your precious future?

ARTHUR
Yes, about my precious future.
Because I highly doubt whether
you and me even have a future...

He exits

13. LATER THAT NIGHT IN HIS APARTMENT

Elizabeth is sitting on the bed drinking a glass of white wine and texting on her phone. She is dressed as if she's about to get out.

ELIZABETH
Hope you had a great time.

ARTHUR
Was alright.

ELIZABETH
Cool!

ARTHUR
Great to see you like that. You
are beautiful.

ELIZABETH
Ah, yeah!

ARTHUR
Going somewhere?

ELIZABETH
Yes.

ARTHUR
OK. Where are you going?

ELIZABETH
Going out to think.

ARTHUR
You don't look like as if you are
just going out to think. You seeing
another guy?

ELIZABETH

Yes!

ARTHUR
Ha, ha, ha, ha great joke.

ELIZABETH
It's not a joke.

ARTHUR
OK well that's it. You´ve obviously lost
your mind. You´re gonna go back to
your druggie friends. I thought so. And,
to tell you the truth, it's an insanity that
you and me could have ever had a
future together. You are just too messed
up in your head.

She throws a glass.

ELIZABETH
I hate you Motherfucker.

ARTHUR
Are you out of your fucking mind?

ELIZABETH
You don't even love me, you don't give a shit
about me.

ARTHUR
You are the most important thing for me.

ELIZABETH
Show me. Fight for me to not get out of this door.

ARTHUR
Why? Give me one reason why? I know the
answer, so you feel better about yourself.

ELIZABETH
So, I can have proof that you love me.

ARTHUR
How much proof do you need? Do you want me
to jump off a cliff?

ELIZABETH
I want to feel that you love me.

ARTHUR
Maybe if you would stop snoring that fucking
coke you would start to feel something.

ELIZABETH
Prove it!!!

ARTHUR
Why? So, you can polish your ego and pay me back
for how wealkings have suppressed and abused
you? It's sick but not hip sick but fucking sick.

ELIZABETH
Why do you love me if I'm so sick for you?

ARTHUR
I love you because deep down in
your heart you are the sanest of
all. I see your beauty and your
passion. Your love to be happy
and creative.

ELIZABETH
You love my ass.

ARTHUR
That too but it's not about your ass.

ELIZABETH
About what is it?

ARTHUR
Again. It's about your heart. It's your
craziness. Your temper, when you're
smiling. It's your will to win.

ELIZABETH
You know you always fall in love
with what you see about yourself
in the other person. I love you.

They kiss

Blackout

14. NEXT MORNING LYING IN BED AT HIS APARTMENT

ARTHUR
Good morning baby.

He reaches over and realizes the bed is empty

                    ARTHUR
          Well that's just great.

Takes out his phone and goes to a porn site and starts masturbating.
Elizabeth comes walking in.

                    ELIZABETH
          What are you doing?

                    ARTHUR
     Jesus!

                    ELIZABETH
          I can't believe it. After last night?

She throws her suitcase in his face.

                    ELIZABETH
          I never want to see you again.

                    ARTHUR
          Come on baby, let's fuck,
          I am doing that because I miss you so much!
          I love you. I want to be with you.
          I want to be the best I can be when you are at your best.

Awkward silence.

                    ELIZABETH
          Oh, baby.....I want us to go far away. I want us to go
          so far away that we can be what we want to be and
          live what we feel and sing anytime we want to sing
          and dance anytime we want to dance. And live free.
          To feel it in every pore.
          To be alive and to feel that what we do matters.

          That we become aware that we can change the world.

                    ARTHUR
          Let's make a difference. That's much more than
          making a baby. I guess. It's like making a baby.

                    ELIZABETH
          Let's make a baby.

She falls into the bed.

1 month later...

15. LATE NIGHT WAKING EACH OTHER UP AT HER APARTMENT

The apartment they are in has no doors. The only one is the front door. There is a numbing low sound that hums throughout the flat.

                    ARTHUR
          I want you to move in with me.

                    ELIZABETH
          What?

                    ARTHUR
          You heard me. I want you to
          come move in with me.

                    ELIZABETH
          Let's talk about this later.

                    ARTHUR
          No let's not talk about this later, let's talk
          about this now.

                    ELIZABETH
          Stop screaming, my children are
          sleeping.

Is seemingly about to lose his mind holding his temper being aware of the responsibility to let her children sleep.

                    ARTHUR
          OK, let's talk like civilized people.

                    ELIZABETH
          Look I want to see the world and the only
          place I want to move to is Los Angeles,
          California.

                    ARTHUR
          What's the difference? I want to go to the
          land of the free, too. But let's find a way to be
          together permanently earlier. I am a man in
          pain here. I need you baby.

                    ELIZABETH
          There will be a lot of things to take into account.
          I am not sure if you're ready for this long lasting
          commitment. I might as well move to another
          city and then be stranded because I trusted you.

> ARTHUR
> You will never be stranded. Where ever you are you gonna find amazing interesting people. You have it all in you.

> ELIZABETH
> It truly sounds too good to be true.

> ARTHUR
> Just give us a chance. All we ever needed was a chance.

> ELIZABETH
> I have to make breakfast for my daughter and bring her to school. We will talk later.

16. IN ARTHUR´S THE APARTMENT

Elisabeth has been doing some work on her computer and Arthur decided to start meditating.

Arthur is meditating Elizabeth enters

> ELIZABETH
> Oh, so you started meditating without me.

Arthur opens his eyes

> ARTHUR
> That doesn't have anything to do with wanting to do it without you but rather with me.

> ELIZABETH
> Ok!

> ARTHUR
> What?

> ELIZABETH
> No it's fine.

> ARTHUR
> What is it now?

> ELIZABETH
> You don't care about me.
> ARTHUR

That's not true.

ELIZABETH
And you want me to come live with you!?

ARTHUR
Yes, I want you to come live with me.
What am I supposed to do?
Waste all that precious time and not
meditate? Let's meditate now.

ELIZABETH
No, I don't want to.

ARTHUR
Now you were saying that you're mad
because I meditate without you and now I
want you to meditate with me and you don't
want to meditate. Tell me what is it exactly
what you want from me?

ELIZABETH
I want you to prove to me that you love me. I
want your soul. Your heart. Your flesh. I
want to see that you are sincere. I want you
to, I want you to...

ARTHUR
Want me to what?

ELIZABETH
Forget it!

ARTHUR
No, tell me.

ELIZABETH
I want you to move in with me.

ARTHUR
OK, that is definitely not going to happen.

ELIZABETH
See you don't give a shit about me.

ARTHUR
You want to get away from here, you said it
yourself. And now you want me to move in
with you to a place you want to get away

from? That doesn't make sense.

ELIZABETH
Yes, it makes sense because it doesn't matter where we are what matters is that we're together.

ARTHUR
Yeah, I know that but what happened to making strong choices? And, you moving away from here proves it to all that you are making these powerful changes.

ELIZABETH
I can´t   deal with this now. Why are you pressuring me? You are pushing me. Stop pushing me!

Phone is ringing

ELIZABETH
I have to take this.

ARTHUR
Great!

She hangs up the phone.

ELIZABETH
OK, where were we?

ARTHUR
Look, I really don't want to pressure you at all. I want you to wake up to your possibilities. You said it yourself. You want to be happy.

ELIZABETH
Yes, I know. I want to be happy with you. I am really sorry I said that you don't love me. Every time I have to give my presentations I feel like I'm all over the place. Please I am sorry. Let's talk later.

She grabs him to bed. Blackout

Act III

17. AT BRUNCHTIME AT HIS APARTMENT

Elisabeth and Arthur have spent the entire day in bed sleeping in. Elisabeth had been preparing food in the kitchen wanting to surprise Arthur bringing him a plate of food to bed. Arthur awakes being alone in bed.

                    ARTHUR
          Well isn't that just great. What a surprise.
          Waiting all day long day in day out, later,
          later, too bad that later never came.

Elizabeth stands in the door holding two plates of food

                    ELIZABETH
          Oh, yeah is that what you think.

She throws the plants against the wall.

                    ARTHUR
          What's the matter with you?

                    ELIZABETH
          I am doing my best here. I want to change. I
          want to do good things for you.

                    ARTHUR
          I understand that.

                    ELIZABETH
          You don't understand shit.

                    ARTHUR
          Baby don't you get it, I want to be with you. I
          want to wake up next to you. To smell you, to
          look into your eyes. I want to see you taking
          proper amounts of rest.

                    ELIZABETH
          You just want to fuck me.

                    ARTHUR
          I want to fuck you yes but it is much more
          than that. I want to see you rise and shine.

   Silence

                    ELIZABETH
          I was preparing that food for two hours.

ARTHUR
Well that's honoring your cooking.

ELIZABETH
Honor, honor, it's all bullshit.

ARTHUR
Relax, come, sit down.

He calms her down sits her on the bed and brings her a
glass of vitamins.

ARTHUR
Drink this.

ELIZABETH
Thank you.

ARTHUR
I love your low-carb pizza.

ELIZABETH
You love yourself.

ARTHUR
Baby, you make me be a better man like in
the movie with Jack Nicholson.

ELIZABETH
Stop doing your charming, I don't know
what.??

ARTHUR
Baby look. You and me, we have everything.

ELIZABETH
I know but how do you enjoy life?

ARTHUR
Through letting go.

ELIZABETH
Ah yeah?

ARTHUR
Just relax baby come on relax and enjoy.

ELIZABETH
I have to work now.

ARTHUR
That's right. Me too actually.

ELIZABETH
You have to work?

ARTHUR
I know it's intense.

ELIZABETH
Dinner at 11?

ARTHUR
Dinner at 11.

18. AT THE DINNER TABLE

The two are sitting at a very large table across from one another. It´s a very middle age touch as if they are dining like king and queen.

ELIZABETH
I love your pumpkin soup.

ARTHUR
Glad you like it.

ELIZABETH
How was your day?

ARTHUR
Productive.

ELIZABETH
What did you do?

ARTHUR
Finishing some stuff I wanted to finish in a long time.

ELIZABETH
Cool!

ARTHUR
4real

ELIZABETH
Look I want to talk about us.

ARTHUR

Sweet

ELIZABETH

I can't deal with your rage. Sometimes you
are so kind and nice and then you have these
outbursts and you don't care how you say it
and you don't care what you are saying and
what you're creating in the other person. You
just drop these bombs and I can't live with
someone who doesn't give me the feeling that
I'm protected.

ARTHUR

I have these outbursts!? Besides, what do
you want me to do? Just bless everything
you do? I'm telling you, you are doing some
fucked up shit.

You know exactly what and then you start with
things like I don't want to bring shame into
your family. It's crazy. I never even said that.

ELIZABETH

I know you. I know people like you. My entire
life I've been with abusive men who cheated
and lied to me. I am sick. I am sick of all
your shit.

ARTHUR

What is it with you? Seriously... Go see a
doctor and get a pill subscription to come to
your senses.

ELIZABETH

You are the one that has to go see a doctor.
You are not normal. You are bipolar. It's sick.
You are fucking sick.

ARTHUR

No, you are the one that sick. I told you
before. Not hip sick but deeply rooted sick.

ELIZABETH

I don't love you.

ARTHUR

OK.

ELIZABETH

I don't love you.

ARTHUR

Well isn't that great. Princess rage is showing
her true face for a change. So, I can get out
now. Finally. Of course, you don't love me. You
are an emotional terrorist and I certainly don't
want to be together with a person like you.

ELIZABETH

What did you say?

ARTHUR

You heard me. You don't even know what
love is.

ELIZABETH

Yeah!?

ARTHUR

Yeah! You have no clue.

ELIZABETH

You're just a little boy. A child.

ARTHUR

I am rather a child then an old woman that is
desperate to feel young again. Guess what
you are fucking old. You wouldn't even see
love if it would grab you by the pussy.

ELIZABETH

I hate you.

ARTHUR

Well fine, you know what? I don't even hate
you because to hate you I must have loved
you once.

Arthur leaves.

19. NEXT DAY IN ARTHUR'S APARTMENT

Arthur is happy because he finally has time to do his morning routine in a long time. He makes a tea. He drinks it. It's like a soothing activity. He recites his forgiveness sentences.

> ARTHUR
> I forgive myself for judging myself as
> someone that doesn't deserve nourishment.
> I forgive myself for judging myself as
> someone that doesn't deserve love and
> loyalty.
> I forgive myself for judging myself as
> someone that can be abused.
> I forgive myself for judging myself as
> someone that is not able to protect the
> people he loves.
> I forgive myself for judging myself as naïve.
> I am light!!!!!!!

He seems reborn. Totally clear. Full of energy. He attempts to sit down to meditate. Elizabeth comes to Arthur´s apartment. She is totally wasted. She has been drinking almost a full bottle of vodka by herself. She is delusional. She slams the door. And speaks gibberish.

> ELIZABETH
> You. Bastard!

> ARTHUR
> How about calling me Jesus. Buddha. Allah.
> Moses. Abraham

> ELIZABETH
> I fucking hate you.

> ARTHUR
> Cool. So you came all the way here just to
> give me this insightful presentation? Are you
> proud of yourself?

> ELIZABETH
> I came here to tell you that I hate you.

> ARTHUR
> Fine. And now?

> ELIZABETH
> You are out of your mind.

He wants to grab the bottle but she pulls it away.

                ELIZABETH
Don't touch me!

                ARTHUR
What is your problem? You are insane!

                ELIZABETH
No. I am   saner than you will ever be!

                ARTHUR
Fuck off! Just fuck off you crazy bitch. Get
out of my life.!

He slams the door.

                ELIZABETH
I hate you I hate you motherfucker.

He sits down on the bed. Blackout

20. ARTHUR WAKES UP: WANTS TO GO TO THE SUPERMARKET

For the first time in months he is calm relaxed and really looking towards a prosperous future. He holds a moment, looks towards the sun. He takes a deep breath says thank you to universe takes his shopping bag and approaches the door to leave. He opens the door and sees her sleeping in front of the doorstep.

ARTHUR

Come on, give me a break .

He grabs her and lays down on the couch.

ELIZABETH

You mother-father !

ARTHUR

What's the matter with you?

ELIZABETH

I hate you.

ARTHUR

I got it. OK? I got it.

ELIZABETH

I love you.

ARTHUR

Well what is it? You hate me then you love
me. The reason you are here is because I
couldn't let you sleep in front of the door like
a homeless person.

ELIZABETH

I am fine. I am only here because the alcohol
made me pass out.
Otherwise, I would be with a real man.

ARTHUR

Look at you. You are such a beautiful woman
but the way you act makes you so ugly I can't
even express how much you
repulse me.

ELIZABETH

You are not normal.

ARTHUR
Are you finished now?

ELIZABETH
Yes, I'm finished now.

ARTHUR
OK, now get the hell out.

ELIZABETH
I'm not going anywhere.

ARTHUR
You are leaving this apartment.

ELIZABETH
I will not leave until you prove to me that you
love me and if I have to take your heart I will
take it.

ARTHUR
What does that even mean, taking my heart?

Beat

ELIZABETH
Look, you made me feel like nobody ever
made me feel before. I want you. I want us. I
have to take care of these things and then
I'm all yours.

ARTHUR
Oh yeah, you're going to take care of your
stuff by getting drunk and passing out in the
middle of the night. Jesus think about your
children.

ELIZABETH
Fuck you, I am a great mother.

ARTHUR
I didn't even say that you are a bad mother.

ELIZABETH
I know exactly what you meant.

ARTHUR
Truth is, you have no clue and you hear what
you want to hear.

ELIZABETH
I know a critic when I see him.

ARTHUR
Well there is constructive criticism and
destructive criticism. What you don't get is
that I actually want to see you win.

ELIZABETH
You want to see me die.

ARTHUR
Ey, shut the fuck up. Wanna see you die,
what a dumb bitch.

He gets up and goes to the bathroom to look himself in
the mirror.

ELIZABETH
Oh, are you gonna lock yourself in the
bathroom again like a little boy who needs
his mama?

ARTHUR
Don't you ever speak about my mother.

ELIZABETH
Oh,, what are you gonna do, you are nothing.

He runs out to the table and grabs the wine bottle

ELIZABETH
No!!!!!

ARTHUR
Oh you want your wine?

ELIZABETH
Give it back.

He rushes to the door throws the bottle outside.

ARTHUR
Go get it!
He runs back into the apartment and shuts the door.

21. THE PHONE CALL

Arthur just made a tea and is about to sit down to meditate. He finally found time to cultivate his consciousness in a long time. Incense is burning and the sun is breaking through the clouds shining on his face. You can see his face is actively losing tension and a light smile appears on his face. He enjoys the silence and the peace of not being bothered for once. Suddenly his phone rings.

ELIZABETH
Can we talk?

ARTHUR
Sure, what is it?

ELIZABETH
Can I come over?

ARTHUR
What, so you can tell me that you hate me?
No thank you.

ELIZABETH
I don't hate you I love you.

ARTHUR
(Sighs) I love you too.

ELIZABETH
Please let me come over it's important.

ARTHUR
OK come over anytime.

ELIZABETH
See you in 10 minutes.

22. AT ARTHUR´S DOOR

Through the phone-call Arthur has been distracted and stopped meditating. He finally gets over his resistance and starts a new attempt to slow down his mind, to let go of the draining circumstances he has with Elisabeth. He sits down and takes a deep breath.

ARTHUR
Finally...

Suddenly the doorbell rings.

ARTHUR

What now!?
Hi, what happened?
You look like you've seen a ghost.

She enters and sits down on the couch.

ARTHUR
Do you want tea?

ELIZABETH
Yes please.

ARTHUR
Green, black, white, mint or chamomile?

ELIZABETH
Green is good.

ARTHUR
OK, what is it?

ELIZABETH
I want us to go far away.

ARTHUR
OK, where do you want to go?

ELIZABETH
I don't care. Far away. I will pay for
everything. I just want you to be with me
and I want to wake up next to you. And
share my life with you. I want to create
with you. I want to feel that you are
sharing the one thing you love most with
me.

ARTHUR

That's a sudden change. Well, why have you been so mean after all the projects we had together? The way we were creating and getting better at what we did was wonderful.

ELIZABETH

Yes, I know. That was just the beginning. I have realized that. I love you because of your art.

Because of the reason you have been fighting all your life to have your own identity.

ARHTUR

Well!

ELIZABETH

Because of your passion I have changed so much and my life has been getting better. I'm living a different life. I can get things done that I wanted to get done for a long time. And, everything works out. With you everything seems easy. I have the power and the strength and even the faith. I love you.

ARTHUR

That's fine, but I can't stand that we are fighting as if we are enemies. As soon as we are talking about something that maters we are fighting. We have so many differences. And maybe it is because we are of a different generation. Let's face it. You could be my mother. And you are clearly traumatized and you don't want to seek professional help. It's not my responsibility to heal you, I have to fix myself.

ELIZABETH

I know that. We know that. Look at the French president. He and his wife have a much greater age difference than we do and they make it work and so we can make it work, too. I believe in it. I believe in us. We are meant to be. Remember you and me?

ARTHUR
I'm not the French president, I am a rockstar.

ELIZABETH
Yes, you are a rockstar.

ARTHUR
I need to think about that. You and me. I know but I have plans for my future and life is not a series of short moments. I want to have a great life and I wanna grow old and successful together with a woman that has compassion and who doesn't only care about herself.

ELIZABETH
I care about you. I´ve never cared about a man like I care about you. You are my world. You're my love. You are the man I want to be with until the rest of my life.

ARTHUR
Sometimes it's really hard to believe that.

ELIZABETH
But it's true. I love you. I want to be your wife.   I want to be your woman. I want to be with you.   I want us to grow old together.

ARTHUR
As soon as things don't go your way you freak out. Your burst and you are so damn hurtful. And I'm the one that saves the relationship by walking after you. Fuck this. Go find yourself someone you can play these games with. How about your ex that treated you like such a slut!? maybe I should treat you like a slut and then you would finally be nicer.

ELIZABETH
I want to change. Please give me another chance. It's so many things at once. And I need to process all this information.

There has been so much change recently
and it's all developing so fast. Sometimes I
think I'm dreaming but I'm not. I love you.

ARTHUR
I have to think about it.

ELIZABETH
What is there to think about? You don't love
me anymore?

ARTHUR
I love you. But I also love myself. I can't
keep up that high pain tolerance. I want
harmony. I don't want to feel pain.
Everything that creates pain in my life will
be replaced. And, that includes you.

ELIZABETH
I want harmony too. I want us to be happy
and powerful together. We are good
together. You know that. You said it
yourself so many times. I see that you have
been fighting for us to be together and now I
want to prove it to you and I'm fighting for
us.

ARTHUR
You want harmony even though you are
projecting from yourself on me. I am this, I
am that, although you are stating all these
things about me that are in fact your flaws.
So, what do you want for me? Do you think
I'm dumb? I can see through you.
You're too proud to surrender to what is
actually going on. You are a coward.

ELIZABETH
I want you. I want us. I want to make it
work. I'm going to seek help. I promise.

ARTHUR
You are just scared to be alone. You're
scared that you're too old and that you will
never find someone else like me. And, the
worst thing is that you never
really show your emotions. I hate it when
you're bitter. I want something emotional
and passionate. You're waiting for me to

break down. Fuck all this shit. I'm sick of
the back-and- forth – and back-and - forth.
All This darkness. I need light.

                    ELIZABETH
I don't know how to react in these
moments. I need time to think, to be alone.
To compensate all of the situations. I am
healing. My life wasn't easy. I have so many
things in my head and to release.

                    ARTHUR
Thank you for your honesty. I need time.
Thank you for coming by and talking about
this. I think it's time for you to go.

        Silence 15 seconds. Intense heartbreaking tension

                    ELIZABETH
I love you.

    She leaves.

23. THE SECOND PHONE CALL

                    ELIZABETH
Can we talk.?

                    ARTHUR
Sure!

                    ELIZABETH
It's something really important. Nothing like before.

                    ARTHUR
What do you mean?

                    ELIZABETH
I've just been to the doctor.

                    ARTHUR
Are you ok?

                    ELIZABETH
I'm coming over.

24. ELIZABETH ENTERS ARTHUR´S APARTMENT

Arthur has been attempting to meditate for all this time but something always distracts him. It seems like that he finally has time to let go to make sense of this whole situation.

> ARTHUR
> Finally...

Instantly the doorbell rings again. He gets up and stops his meditation, again.

> ARTHUR
> Well I guess not.
> Okay, tell me.

> ELIZABETH
> I'm pregnant. He spits out his drink.

> ARTHUR
> What? I thought you are taking the baby pill!!!!!

> ELIZABETH
> I told you that I stopped taking it.

Arthur breaks down. He is entering a dreamlike state, keeps rocking back and forth. She knees down to him wanting to catch his attention.

> ELIZABETH
> Everything will be fine after the wedding.

Arthur is fantasizing as if he is speaking with a ghost. Laughing and being terrified at the same time. A voodoo spirit is appearing. He just looks in mistrust and delusion.

> ELIZABETH
> Kuck kuck... wedding.

Elisabeth walks back and forth wanting to get his attention.

> ELIZABETH
> Answer me you prick.

Arthur is not responding

> ELIZABETH
> Okay whatever. I am not pregnant.
> But I can tell you what I want. You are so gullible.

Arthur breaks out of the trance. The voodoo creature bursts into a billion pieces by a light from within.

> ARTHUR
> The power of Christ, compels you.

Instantly a loud bang. A flash-bang and cops are running in with machine guns. Everything goes into slow-motion.

> SWAT OFFICER
> Lilitu Zora* ...You are under arrest for sham weddings in 10 states. ... Sir, you are a lucky man.
> (* the one that steals energy from men while they are asleep)

> ARTHUR
> Lilitu Zora? Who the hell is Lilitu Zora?

> SWAT OFFICER
> Well, that's her real name.

Arthur is looking with disbelief. He closes his eyes, takes a breath, turns his head towards the sun, opens his eyes, and looks at her.

> ARTHUR
> The power of Christ compels you!

The officers arrest Lilitu and leave. Arthur stays back alone. Time passes in slow motion again. The sun shines even brighter than before. Suddenly the room turns dark and the sun disappears. Intimidating darkness. Instantly a spotlight on the piano with the sound of a harp. He plays the final song.

THE END

Printed in Great Britain
by Amazon

81625659R00032